Family

Here is Tiana.
She has a family.

Here is Naveen.
He has a family.

Here is Tiana's mother.
She has a family.

Here is Naveen's mother.
She has a family.

Here is Naveen's father.
He has a family.

Here is Naveen's brother.
He has a family.

They are a family.